song of the boat

pictures by
Leo and Diane Dillon

song of the boat

Lorenz Graham

THOMAS Y. CROWELL COMPANY, NEW YORK

By Lorenz Graham

DAVID HE NO FEAR
EVERY MAN HEART LAY DOWN
GOD WASH THE WORLD AND START AGAIN
HONGRY CATCH THE FOOLISH BOY
A ROAD DOWN IN THE SEA
SONG OF THE BOAT

Library of Congress Cataloging in Publication Data
Graham, Lorenz B.   Song of the boat.
SUMMARY: A small African boy helps his father locate the right tree to make a new canoe to replace the one broken by an alligator. [1. Africa—Fiction] I. Dillon, Leo, illus. II. Dillon, Diane, illus. III. Title. PZ7.G7577So   [E]   74-5183 ISBN 0-690-75231-8, ISBN 0-690-75232-6 (lib. bdg.)

1   2   3   4   5   6   7   8   9   10

In Africa there are many nations or tribes. The people of each tribe speak their own language. In West Africa the language might be Mandingo or Kru or Yoruba or Ibo.

But many of the people have learned to speak English. Those who have been to school have large vocabularies and they follow strict rules of grammar. Others speak a simple form. To the English they bring vivid poetry and strong rhythm.

This is the story of an African villager, Flumbo by name, who has lost his boat in a fight with an alligator, and of his son, Momolu, who helped his father get a new boat. It is told in the folk speech of the people there.

Flumbo walk about in Bonga Town.
He say How-Do to everybody,
But him heart no lay down, cause he no got boat.
Alligator did break him canoe.

All the people know Flumbo and they like him.
Flumbo be strong. He be strong past them other men.
He strong and he good.
The people like him plenty.

When Flumbo go for waterside,
Plenty people say to him,
"Oh, this time you no got canoe;
So now you go in my canoe;
Make it my canoe be same way for your own canoe."

Flumbo say, "No!" and he laugh.
Flumbo say, "If Flumbo take other man canoe,
By and by alligator going break him,
Same way alligator did break my own."
Flumbo laugh for him mouth.
But Flumbo no laugh for him heart.

Soon one morning Flumbo rise up, and he say,
"Now I go find my canoe."
He pick up cutlass, and he pick up axe.
Him woman, Portee, she fix small chop in clean cloth,
And Momolu, him small boy, pick up the chop.

Flumbo look him small boy.
He say, "The road I walk be long. Oh,
It be long past the legs of my small boy."
Momolu look up and he say,
"Elephant cross big hill;
Goat cross big hill same way."

And so all two go.
Flumbo walk plenty. Momolu walk behind.
All two walk by the river,
And if they leave one river,
Soon they walk by another river.

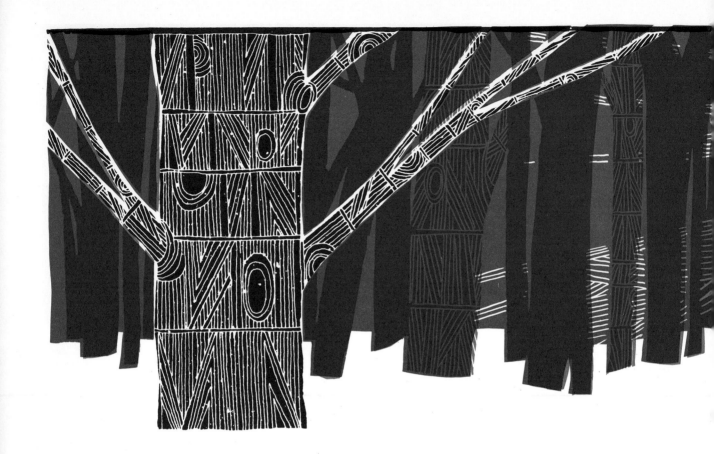

When Flumbo see a black gum tree,
He look him good.
Some tree be too big.
Some tree be too small.
Some tree no be straight.
Some tree no be clean.
No tree seem right for fine canoe.

By and by Momolu be tired,
But he no say one word self.
By and by sun stand overhead,
And Momolu have hunger.

Now Momolu say, "Leg be strong past belly;
Leg say 'go,' belly say 'stop.'
How say my pa now?"
Flumbo say, "Belly got sense."

All two sit down by small river.
All two take chop.
All two eat boiled cassava
And ground peas and sweet oranges.
All two rest.
All two tired.
All two sleep.

Momolu hear somebody call him name:
"Momolu! Momolu!"
Momolu say, "Who call Momolu?"
Momolu hear again.
"Momolu! Momolu! Come with me."

Momolu rise up and go.
Momolu no savvy the way he go.
Momolu no savvy the place he go.
Momolu just go.

Momolu hear people laugh.
He hear them say, "Here is Momolu!
Now our hearts lay down
Cause our good friend did come."

Momolu say, "Now I hear your word,
But I no see your face.
What side you live?"
The people say, "Open your eyes."
Momolu open him eyes, and Momolu see.

He see people who be like no other people.
They be happy past all other people.
When they talk, the talk be like song.
When they walk, they go softly softly in the air,
And they no get tired.

The people say, "This time we show you. Come!"
Momolu go along same way in the air.
By and by the people say, "Now you see canoe!"
Momolu see one fine tree, fine past all he ever see before.

And while he look, the tree become a canoe.
And while he look some more, the canoe become a tree.
Momolu say, "Now I see!"

Momolu hear Flumbo say, "Come, we go!"
Momolu say, "Wait, Pa, I see your canoe."
Then Momolu wake up and he savvy.
He savvy that it be a dream.
He tell him pa.

Flumbo say, "Ahanh! Come, we go!
Now my small boy walk in front,
And I go walk behind him."

Momolu walk.
He no savvy the way he go.
He no savvy why he go that place.
By and by he stop by that same fine tree.
Flumbo say, "I see my canoe!
It live inside this tree."

For many days Flumbo bring something for the tree.
A day he bring a country cloth,
Blue with small white lines.
He wrap it round the tree.
A day he put down by the tree a bright brass pan.
He cook new rice and put it in the pan.
A day he bring palm wine, a heavy gourd of wine.
He pour it on the ground;
Under the gumwood tree he pour out all the wine.

And then one day
Bomokoko, the priest, did come
With all the people of the town.
The drummers beat their drums,

And Bomokoko call the spirit of the tree.
The singers sing. The dancers dance.
And by and by the spirit say
The canoe be for Flumbo.

Plenty days Flumbo come.
He cut. He cut. He cut.
By and by the tree fall down.
Plenty days again Flumbo cut.
He cut. He cut. He cut.
By and by he make one piece.

Plenty days again Flumbo cut
For make a shape, for make sharp end,
For make round bottom, for make inside,
For make seat, for make even, for make clean.
By and by canoe be finished.

All the people come for see.
All the people say, "Oh!
Flumbo did make fine canoe, fine past all canoes!"
Flumbo say, "My small boy did find this canoe for me."
All the people no savvy.

Now they go for ride.
Flumbo sit in back, and he paddle.
Momolu sit in front, and he beat him drum and sing.
Portee sit between,
And Portee happy too much.
She happy cause her man make a canoe.
She happy, too, cause her small boy make a song.
Hear the song of the boat.
Hear the song that Momolu did sing:
    "Flumbo make a fine canoe.
    Flumbo make a fine canoe.
    Flumbo make a fine canoe,
    And the water is loving it too."

About the Author

Lorenz Graham was born in New Orleans, Louisiana. His father was a minister, and his childhood was spent in a succession of different parsonages. After graduation from high school in Seattle, Washington, the author attended the University of California in Los Angeles. In his third year, however, he left college to become a teacher at a mission school in Africa.

The great disparity between the American idea of Africa and the reality of African life first prompted Mr. Graham's interest in writing for young people. On his return to the United States, the author was graduated from Virginia Union University, and he later did postgraduate work at the New York School for Social Work and at New York University.

Lorenz Graham likes working directly with people and their problems. He has been a social worker and a probation officer. Most of his time is now given over to his writing.

While in Africa, Mr. Graham met his wife, who was also a teacher. They make their home in southern California.

About the Artists

Leo and Diane Dillon met when they were students at the Parsons School of Design, and they married shortly after graduation. They have also both attended and taught at the School of Visual Arts in New York City. They bring years of study of native arts and crafts to their book design and illustration, and they refuse to be restricted to any one technique or style. The Dillons live and work in their remodelled brownstone house in Brooklyn, New York, with their young son, Leo, who is a passionate student of the guitar.